MUSLIM CHILDREN'S LIBRARY

A School Girl's Hero
Author: Umm Aamina
Illustrator: Kulthum Burgess
Book Design: Stevan Stratford
Co-ordinator: Anwar Cara

Published by
The Islamic Foundation
Markfield Conference Centre
Ratby Lane, Markfield
Leicestershire, LE67 9SY
United Kingdom
T (01530) 244 944
F (01530) 244 946
E publications@islamic-foundation.org.uk

Quran House, PO Box 30611, Nairobi, Kenya
PMB 3193, Kano, Nigeria

Distributed by Kube Publishing

British Library Cataloguing in Publication Data
    Aamina, Umm
    A school girl's hero. - (Muslim children's library)
    1. Heroes - Juvenile fiction 2. Muslim girls - Fiction 3. School contests - Juvenile
fiction 4. Didactic fiction 5. Children's stories
    I. Title II. Burgess, Kulthum III. Islamic Foundation (Great Britain) 823.9'2[J]
ISBN-13: 9780860374213

Printed by Proost International Book Production, Belgium

A SCHOOL GIRL'S HERO

Umm Aamina

Illustrated by Kulthum Burgess

Acknowledgments:
A story inspired by my wonderful nieces and nephew, Anum, Samah and Saif-Ullah.
May they be gifted with the best of character, so that they too are an inspiration to
others. *Ameen*

Dring, Dring, Dring went the morning school bell. Anum, Samah and Saif all said Salam to their mummy, during the hustle and bustle before school began. Samah as always ran through the school gates, full of energy and raring to go. Anum and Saif however, were always reluctant to return to school after the weekend. They had all started a new school this year and it had taken Anum quite some time to get used to it. She missed her old school friends.

Monday this term was especially difficult for Anum. Not only did the weekend fly past, as always, but it was 'THE DREADED SWIMMING DAY'. Having always been quite prim and proper since a toddler and knowing about 'accidents' in the pool, she found swimming pretty gross. She was far from a natural swimmer, and to add insult to injury her teacher insisted on calling her a 'Little Mermaid'. As if this couldn't be any further from the truth, Anum would think. "*As-Salamu 'Alaykum*, Anum," greeted Doha as Anum sat down next to her. "*Wa 'Alaykum as-Salam Warahmatullah*," replied Anum not looking very happy.

"Dreading swimming?" asked Doha.

"Ahuh, especially after last week. I mean why would any teacher make a child like ME who can only just about doggy paddle, jump into the deep end," said Anum feeling agitated.

"Yeh, but you did have a pole to hold onto, and anyway you did do it," said Rebecca, another friend of Anum's.

"I suppose, but I felt as if I had drunk half of the pool, and just thinking about it makes me feel sick," said Anum whilst slowly turning quite grey in colour.

"Siiiiiiileeeeeeeeeence…..Thank you and good morning everyone." Mrs Thorn had entered the classroom. She definitely was a teacher who ensured that the children behaved, but was also very much liked by all the class.

"I'm afraid I have some bad news…" then she paused and raised her pointy eyebrows at Anum, "…or maybe good news for some. Swimming has been cancelled today due to renovations at the leisure centre, so we'll be having a double English session instead."
Amidst the booing and whining was an excited, "yes, yes, yes".
"I thought you'd feel like that Anum," said Mrs Thorn giving Anum a huge smile.

"Did you hear that, no swimming and even better double English. *Al-Hamdulillah*," sighed Anum and some colour instantly came to her face.

She absolutely loved writing and using her imagination, and of course with the added bonus of getting good marks, today seemed to be getting better and better.

"I'd like to tell you about a competition for English that years four, five and six will be participating in. A prize of fifty pounds will be awarded to a child from each year. PLUS their piece of work will be published in the local newspaper," said Mrs Thorn.

"What do we have to do though Miss, what do we have to dooo?" said Brian impatiently with his bottom hovering over his chair.

"I would like you to write about who you want to be like with an explanation of why. The title of your work is 'Who I aspire to be like'," wrote Mrs Thorn on the blackboard.

There was a real sense of excitement in the class, and the children started shouting out names of who they admire. There were names of actors, actresses, models, pop stars, and all so, so predictable, thought Anum.

"Like you, Miss," said Natasha.
"Oh please, as if the other suggestions weren't bad enough," said Doha.
"I need to vomit," said Rebecca.
"Ok let's not be horrible," said Anum feeling guilty.

"I want to be like my cat Kitty," said Rebecca confidently.
"Shhhhh, someone may hear you and they'll never let you
forget it." Anum quietened her down.
"Can you imagine the names, Kitteeeeey, here Kitty Kitty
Kitty, and cat girl, whiskas, meeeooooooow," said Doha looking
at Rebecca oddly.

"I don't care what anyone else thinks, and anyway it's not the whiskers or tail that I want. It's the warmth and happiness that Kitty gives that I'd like to give to others. Cats are grateful especially my Kitty. She's so easily pleased. All she needs is a few hugs, some milk, and food scooped from a tin. Cats don't think about what you look like, where you come from, or how you dress. As long as you're kind to them, they're happy with you however you are. Nowadays you would be lucky to find these qualities in humans."

Anum and Doha sat staring at Rebecca, who had defended her idea so well. They realised now how impressed they actually were, and so gave her lots of encouragement for her originality.

"Come on, Anum, you take so long," whined Saif, whilst he waited with his mum and Samah in the playground.
"I'm coming," smiled Anum.
"I know why you're smiling. It's because swimming was cancelled wasn't it?" asked Samah.
Anum laughed.

That evening after dinner together as a family, they all sat in the living room. The children were playing, doing their homework or chatting with their parents. Their father would always ask what they did at school and how their day was. Saif, the youngest of the three gave his usual reply, "I can't remember."
Samah on the other hand in her usual bright manner gave an exciting summary of what she did, straight to the point.
Anum then told them all about the school competition.

"I know, you can write about me, I'm an excellent footballer," said Saif.

"No Saif, Anum doesn't want to be a footballer does she?" said Samah.

"Why not?" said Saif surprised.

"Anyway," nodded Saif dismissing what Samah had to say "you have to win because I want to help you spend the prize."

Anum and Samah broke out into giggles, "Oh Saifey."

For the next couple of days the same question continued puzzling Anum: 'Who do I aspire to be like?' Then, whilst she was busy helping her mum with chores it suddenly came to her. It now seemed so obvious, and she couldn't believe it hadn't come to her earlier. She told her family about her idea and they were all really impressed, but Anum then began having second thoughts. She knew nobody else would write about this person, and was worried about what the teacher and other children would think. Certain children in the class would definitely laugh at her.

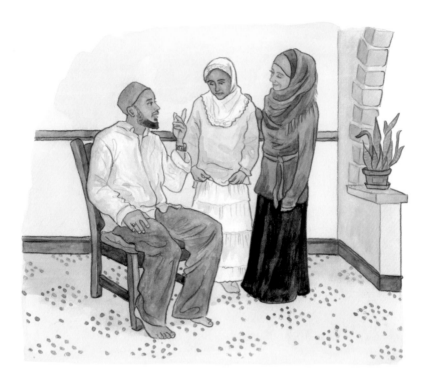

"Do it, do it, do it," chanted Samah and Saif.

Anum appreciated Samah and Saif's support, but it wasn't quite what she needed.

"Anum, remember that Muslims should always be truthful. So if this is the person you want to be like, then you should trust Allah and write about him," said Anum's father, making it sound so simple.

"That's right! Also, when we say '*Iyyaka na'budu wa iyyaka nasta'in*' from *Surah al-Fatihah* we are saying that we worship Allah and ask for His help. So seek His help and you'll be fine," added Anum's mother.

Anum felt so reassured by her parent's advice, and always appreciated their reminders to trust in Allah. It truly made every task so much easier.

The following weekend Anum began her research for the competition. There was so much information it was difficult sifting through it all, but Anum persevered.

Every day at school the hot topic of conversation seemed to be the competition, and most children had completed their entries. Anum, quite the perfectionist, continued making her changes until the night before the deadline. The person Anum aspired to be like was very special, and just so perfect through her eyes. If only people came to know about this person they too would want to know more, thought Anum. Maybe they could learn from the beautiful way through which this person changed the world for the better. By winning this competition this is my opportunity to tell lots of people about my hero. Anum was now feeling very determined.

It was *Jumu'ah*, a mini Eid was how her mother would describe
it, and today was the deadline for the competition.
"As-Salamu 'Alaykum warahmatullah" recited Anum's father,
as he completed the *Fajr* prayer with the family in
jama'at. Anum prostrated knowing that this was the closest she
could be to Allah, and made a *du'a*:
"Oh Allah, please, please, please, let the person I aspire to be
like be an inspiration to all those in my school. Please let none
of the children make fun of me, and help me to be brave.
Hasbunallahu wa ni'mal wakil (Allah is enough for us and He is
the Best Guardian). *Ameen.*"

Dong, Dong, Dong echoed the second bell for school.
Anum sat on her chair feeling quite nervous. Rebecca, however,
despite her hero being her cat was so excited. If she was given
the opportunity, she would read out her entry there and then.
"Today is the deadline for the essay competition," shouted Mrs
Thorn waking Anum from deep thought.
Everyone placed their essays into the homework box on Mrs
Thorn's desk. There were some children in the class who were
very confident that they would win.
"You've all wasted your time as mine is a guaranteed winner,"
said Marie smugly.
Boy does she annoy me, thought Anum.

Anum had not told anyone in the class who she had written about except Doha and Rebecca, as she trusted them. Doha was especially impressed and told Anum that it was an 'ace idea'.

Friday 21st of May, a date Anum knew she'd never forget, and one that felt as if it would never arrive. Today was the school assembly, in which the winners of the competition were to be announced. The winners would then read their entries out to the assembly.
Parents of the school children had been invited, so the school's main hall was bursting with people. The attendance was the greatest the school had ever seen. It was clearly a lot more than Mrs Mann, the headmistress had expected.
"So many parents but all very welcome," she said squashing the children closer and closer like sardines in a tin.
Anum's parents had their video camera as always, and Samah and Saif sat excitedly on the floor, each with their class group.
Anum on the other hand felt very nervous. Her hands were

especially clammy, despite playing her parents reassuring words in her mind again and again.

"Good morning! I would like to welcome you all to a very special assembly. Today we have invited parents to listen to some very impressive pieces of writing and…"

Mrs Mann continued with details of the 'Who I aspire to be like' competition.

The winners would be announced beginning with Anum's year, and then working up to the senior years. Anum felt relieved that her year was first, otherwise her already very stretched sleeves would have had no elasticity left. Mrs Mann spoke of how impressed the panel of judges had been, and how difficult it had been to choose a single winner. Hence, they chose two runners up which were on display at the back of the hall.

"Now is the time to announce the winner from year three." Anum's year. The children began chattering and there was even hand drumming on the floor, as an attempt to build up

the excitement. Mrs Mann soon calmed things down to the pin drop silence that she liked.

"The award goes to…" then she paused "…Anum Khan."

There were claps and cheering and Anum heard Saif shouting, "That's my sister, and she's really brainy."

After realising that her ears had not made a mistake, Anum felt her face going beetroot in colour. She was not quite sure what to do next.

"Go on, Anum. Mrs Mann is calling you, *Masha' Allah* you've won," said Doha trying to hug Anum, though it felt like a strangle.

Anum stepped out of the audience, and as she turned to face everyone she could feel her legs going wobbly. Then, upon seeing her parents who looked so proud, Anum began to feel a lot better.

She quietly recited the du'a that her mother had taught her since she was young:

Rabbishrahli sadri wa yassirli amri wahlul uqdatan min lisani yafqahu qawli.

(Oh Lord, open my heart for me, and make my task easy, and take away my difficulty in speaking, so that they may understand what I say).

Anum then read her winning piece.

Who do I aspire to be like?

Who do I aspire to be like?; I had been asking myself for several days. A pop star, a film actress, no all that was not for me. Nelson Mandela a man who has spent years struggling for equality. Hmmmm, now I was getting warmer, but I was still not quite sure. There are so many other qualities that I would like to have and so I continued with my search.

Dont you hate it when you are punished when you havent done something wrong. I was told off in the playground the other day, as another child said I pushed into the queue at the water fountain. There were others there who knew that I hadn't but didn't have the courage to speak up. Speaking up and not allowing others to be treated unfairly can be difficult, but is so important so let me tell you why.

Then, one day when taking some food that my mummy had cooked to a sick neighbour, it came to me in seconds. It was as if the answer had always been there, and it now seemed so obvious. Why had it taken so long I thought to myself, and then I realised. I wanted to fit in with most of the other children in my class, and being a little different felt quite scary. I can't possibly write about this person…what will everyone at school think…will they laugh at me? After a lot of worrying I have decided that being different makes the world interesting, and I have built up the courage to be honest.

I aspire to be like someone who is definitely no pop star or film actor, and probably unheard of by many. But, for me he is a very special person with wonderful qualities. During his life he showed people a different way to live. He is an example that I know I have learnt lots from, and hope others can too, and so I begin.

Don't you hate it when you're treated unfairly, especially if you're punished when you haven't done anything wrong. I was told off in the playground the other day, as another child said I had pushed into the queue at the water fountain. There were others there who knew that I hadn't but didn't have the courage to speak up. Speaking up and not allowing others to be treated unfairly can be difficult, but is so important so let me tell you why.

Imagine a tiny new-born baby whose mummy holds her for the first time ever, but that first time is the last time. The baby is then taken away and buried whilst still breathing, but why? …simply because she is a girl! The man I aspire to be like grew up in a place where this was normal and happened all the time, and only *he* had the courage to speak up and make a change. The change he made goes like this…

Now imagine that tiny new-born baby whose mother holds her for the first time ever, and she can be sure of being hugged and kissed many times over. Had she been a boy she would have been seen as no better, but equal, a baby girl with a happy future. This is how I'd like to be, where even if all the people I love cannot see the bad things that are happening, I speak up when others need my help so that we're all treated fairly.

This special person also teaches me about the important things to look for when choosing our friends. Sometimes we choose our friends because of the way they look, the clothes they wear or how popular they are in the class. So, sometimes when these friends use bad language, bully and call names, we join in or watch silently, maybe because we want to fit in and know that otherwise we could be at the receiving end. 'Nigger' if you're black, 'Paki' if you're brown and 'Honkey' if you're white, and if you're not trendy then you could be in for a rough ride. Why is it so wrong to look different? Wouldn't our world be so boring if we were all the same? This man teaches me that when we make friends it's not the outside that's important but the inside, so a good character is now number one on my list.

A lot of us have nick-names; some not as nice as others, and some like mine which get a bit embarrassing as you get older. But have you ever heard someone being nick-named 'Trustworthy' or 'Honest'? This was the nick-name of this person, which seems a bit strange to me as I'm used to hearing things like 'Liar'. Imagine if the grown-ups were trying to sort something out, and they then called for your help because you were so truthful! This is exactly what would happen to him. Lying and telling other people's secrets sometimes seem to slip out so easily, but slowly we would lose lots of our friends as they would not be able to trust us.

There are so many other things about this man that I want to tell you, even the little things like 'a smile is charity'. When we usually think of giving charity we rummage into our pockets for money or search through our toys for something nice. But we forget that all these things have something in common, as they make  people happy. This is why even a smile can be charity, as I know that every time my baby brother smiles at me it makes me feel so happy.

This man would help the poor and orphans because he cared and was trying to share a special message. So here I am asking myself, "Do I want to win this competition for the prize, or do I truly want to share a message, to try and make our world better?"

So, this is what I aspire to be like, and this message is how I want our world to be. Maybe you have guessed who he is? Well his name is Muhammad (peace and blessings be upon him), and he was the last Prophet of Islam, and his message is the Qur'an.

The End
By Anum Khan

Anum had read her work with such enthusiasm, and what she had written clearly came straight from the heart. Many parents and teachers were so moved by her words, that their eyes were filled with tears. The school hall in which there was only Anum's voice, then changed to an overwhelming applause. Anum stood blushing with embarrassment.

Within a couple of weeks Anum's story was published in the local newspaper, which her parents framed for her as a gift.

Anum had learnt from the school competition that even if people were not of the same faith, Allah has created us with some common moral values. It also showed her how the Prophet's message was still as special now as it was when he was alive, and how it can work for us even today.

A School Girl's Hero

Competition Winner Anum With a Message For The Whole World

· Anum and her proud father ·